# The Disappearing Island

*For Temi, Matt, and Betsy* ⌒ *C. D.*

*For Judith Whipple* ⌒ *T. L.*

*Acknowledgments*
*The author wishes to thank the Wellfleet Historical Society,*
*the Wellfleet Public Library, and Cape Cod National Seashore.*

**ARTIST'S NOTE:** Using a 7H pencil, I make a very detailed final pencil drawing on a sheet of Strathmore 500 Bristol. Only when this drawing is exactly right do I begin applying the watercolor. I use Winsor & Newton tube watercolors and #3 and #10 red sable brushes. The paper is taped to a board and laid flat on my drawing table. I paint quickly and directly, rarely reworking areas. This keeps the colors clear and bright.

SIMON & SCHUSTER BOOKS FOR YOUNG READERS
An imprint of Simon & Schuster Children's Publishing Division
1230 Avenue of the Americas, New York, New York 10020
Text copyright © 2000 by Corinne Demas. Illustrations copyright © 2000 by Ted Lewin, Ltd.
All rights reserved including the right of reproduction in whole or in part in any form.
SIMON & SCHUSTER BOOKS FOR YOUNG READERS is a trademark of Simon & Schuster.
Book design by Lily Malcom. The text for this book is set in Garamond.
Printed in Hong Kong
2 4 6 8 10 9 7 5 3 1
Library of Congress Cataloging-in-Publication Data: Demas, Corinne.
The disappearing island / by Corinne Demas ; illustrated by Ted Lewin. — 1st ed.
p.   cm.
Summary: To celebrate her ninth birthday, Carrie's grandmother takes her by boat to
Billingsgate Island off Cape Cod, an island that is visible only during low tides.
ISBN 0-689-80539-X
[1. Cape Cod (Mass.)—Fiction. 2. Islands—Fiction. 3. Tides—Fiction. 4. Grandmothers—Fiction.
5. Birthdays—Fiction.] I. Lewin, Ted, ill. II. Title.
PZ7.B61917Di 2000
[E]—dc21
98-37733
CIP   AC

# The
# Disappearing Island

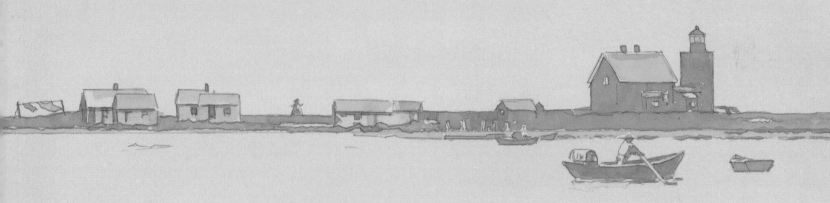

By Corinne Demas

Illustrated by Ted Lewin

Simon & Schuster Books for Young Readers

For my ninth birthday my grandma gave me a small box. Inside was a perfect sand dollar and a note. The note said:

> To celebrate your birthday we will voyage out to the disappearing island
> where I found this sand dollar when I was just your age.

"How can an island disappear?" I asked.

Grandma laughed. "When I take you out to Billingsgate Island, Carrie, you'll see," she said.

I'd been all around Wellfleet Harbor in Grandma's boat, but this time we were going to go farther out, into Cape Cod Bay, just the two of us, farther than I'd ever been before.

Grandma's boat is named *Aphrodite*, after the goddess of love who first rose out of the sea foam. It's painted the blue of the sea on the outside and the blue of the sky on the inside.

The next day we rowed out to *Aphrodite* in a rubber boat so small our legs were in a tangle.

We clambered aboard *Aphrodite,* and Grandma hooked the rubber boat to the mooring. To get the old outboard motor started she had to pull the rope nearly ten times. Her arms are all muscles from clamming and swimming and pulling. We put on our life jackets, and I sat up on the bow and pretended I was a figurehead on one of the old ships that used to come into Wellfleet Harbor. Water sprayed me, but it was a hot day so I didn't mind.

When the tide is high in Wellfleet Harbor, the water is way over my head. When the tide is low, it just comes up to my middle. Grandma has a tide chart on her wall. It's like a calendar for the sea. There's low tide and high tide twice a day, and every day it's an hour different. The tide was going out now. A cormorant was drying out its feathers on a rock that hadn't been there an hour before. When we rode out beyond the sheltered part of Wellfleet Harbor, the waves got higher and I went to sit in the back of the boat with Grandma.

"I don't see any island," I said.

She passed me the binoculars. "Keep looking straight ahead," she told me. "At high tide it is completely covered by water. It begins to appear as the tide goes out."

Finally we got close enough so I could see it: a flat stretch of beach out in the middle of the sea. We pulled into a cove, and Grandma anchored *Aphrodite*. We waded to shore, carrying our lunch basket and beach blanket.

We laid out the blanket on a high sandy spot surrounded by rocks—the foundation for the old lighthouse, Grandma said. Then we went off to explore the island.

There were no buildings, no trees, not even a blade of grass. Just sand. The sand was all in long ripples made by the waves as the tide had gone out. I ran as far as I could run without stopping to catch my breath. Grandma ran beside me.

"A century ago, this island was a mile long," Grandma explained. "This was a busy fishing community, and there were thirty-five homes here and a school. There were meadows and gardens. When the sea started eroding the island, people moved off and took their houses with them. When I was a little girl, my dad used to take me out here to go clamming. There was more of the island than there is now, but no one lived here anymore."

We were the only ones on the island except for the gulls and the terns. There were shells everywhere: jingle shells and quahogs, razor clams and channeled whelks. Mussels, tiny as ants, covered the stones in the acres of tidal pools. They looked like black fur.

I found a broken brick, half buried in the sand. One side of it had been charred.

"This was from someone's chimney," Grandma said.

"May I keep it?"

"Sure. The sea would claim it soon enough."

We hiked back to our blanket, and nearby I saw a strange, rusty creature that looked like the backbone of a whale.

"It's the metal spiral staircase from the old lighthouse, lying on its side," Grandma told me. It was too big for us to carry back to safety on the mainland.

"That was the second lighthouse out here. The first one toppled into the sea. They built this one farther inland and they built it out of brick. They thought it would last forever, but the sea kept taking more and more of the island. They built a big breakwater out of rocks, but the sea just came around it."

Grandma pointed to a curve of gray rocks that were covered with barnacles that looked like white lace.

"That's what's left of the breakwater," she said. "Just around the time I was born, the last lighthouse keeper moved off the island. They built a tower with an automatic light, and that winter the big brick lighthouse was knocked down by the sea in a storm. Now, the light tower is gone as well."

I lay back on the blanket and closed my eyes. The hot sun made everything swimming and orange under my lids. While I listened to Grandma talk, I imagined it was a hundred years ago.

*I've come to the island to visit my friend whose father is the lighthouse keeper. They live in the brick house that is attached to the lighthouse. She comes running to meet my boat with her little dog barking at her heels.*

*In the yard there are some well-fed pigs, a flock of chickens, and a nasty rooster who thinks he owns the whole island. In the garden beside the house the tomatoes are as red as the lobster buoys piled by the dory on the beach. There are roses growing by the doorway and bees humming in the lavender.*

*Inside the lighthouse it is cool as a cave. It takes a while for my eyes to adjust to the darkness. We climb up the spiral staircase to the top of the lighthouse and step outside into the glimmering sunshine on the walkway that circles the great lamp. I can see to Province-town and beyond. I can see as far as anyone has ever seen before. Ships with sails as white as my summer dress are making their way along the horizon. The rooster, who is practicing for sunrise, starts to crow.*

A rooster *was* crowing. I opened my eyes. But it wasn't a rooster, it was a herring gull who thought he owned the island.

In the basket Grandma had packed sandwiches and leftover birthday cake from my party the day before. She lit a candle, and the wind and I blew it out together. Grandma sang "Happy Birthday Plus One."

"Someday," she said, "this island will be completely gone, and you'll tell your granddaughter how you came out here and picnicked on it at low tide."

"I'll show her the brick as proof," I said.

Now the tide was coming back in. It moved slowly at first, as if making up its mind, and then it started claiming the edges of the beach.

Grandma stroked the smooth sand beside her.

"In this modern world people can do almost anything," she said. "We cut canals and build long bridges and dam rivers. We've tamed almost everything. I'm glad that we haven't completely tamed the ocean, too. What I love about a place like this is that it reminds us that nature still can have its way once in a while."

Grandma stood up. "Time to get going," she said.

We each took a corner of the beach blanket and let it flap free of sand in the wind. Then we folded the blanket together, like partners in a square dance. When our hands came together, Grandma kissed my knuckles and my nose.

The tide was coming in faster now, eating up the beach, eating up the island. We waded out to *Aphrodite*. Grandma started the engine in two tries, and we went chugging off. I looked back as Billingsgate Island began to disappear in the distance, and in the sea. The spot where Grandma and I had had our picnic would soon be underwater. Where the chickens once pecked for grain thrown out by the lighthouse keeper's little girl a hundred years ago, fish would peck at plankton.

By the time *Aphrodite* was back at her mooring in Wellfleet Harbor, Billingsgate Island was gone, a secret beneath the waves.

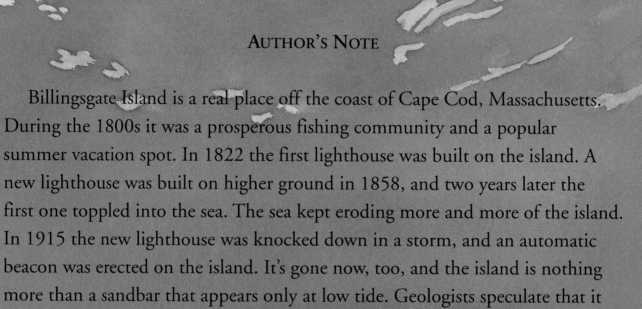

## AUTHOR'S NOTE

Billingsgate Island is a real place off the coast of Cape Cod, Massachusetts. During the 1800s it was a prosperous fishing community and a popular summer vacation spot. In 1822 the first lighthouse was built on the island. A new lighthouse was built on higher ground in 1858, and two years later the first one toppled into the sea. The sea kept eroding more and more of the island. In 1915 the new lighthouse was knocked down in a storm, and an automatic beacon was erected on the island. It's gone now, too, and the island is nothing more than a sandbar that appears only at low tide. Geologists speculate that it won't be around for long.

Billingsgate Island isn't the only island in the world that's disappearing or has disappeared. The legendary island of Atlantis, first written about by Plato, was supposed to have been a great ancient empire that sank into the Atlantic Ocean. Many people over the centuries have hunted for traces of Atlantis. Some people think Plato's Atlantis was mere myth; others believe Plato based his story on a real place. Some scientists have argued that Atlantis was part of the Island of Thera, which was destroyed in 1500 B.C. by an erupting volcano.